UNDER ATTACK

JIM ELDRIDGE

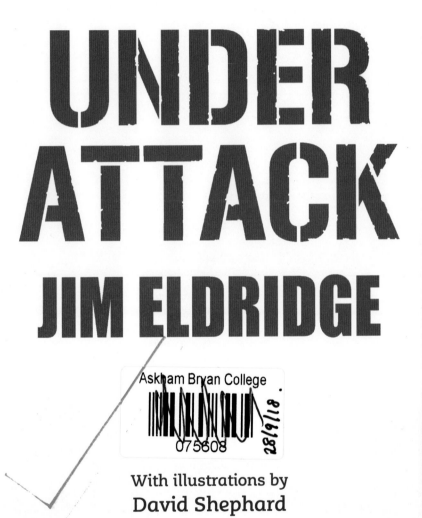

With illustrations by
David Shephard

Barrington Stoke

To Lynne, my inspiration

First published in 2013 in Great Britain by
Barrington Stoke Ltd
18 Walker Street, Edinburgh, EH3 7LP

www.barringtonstoke.co.uk

Reprinted 2018

Text © 2013 Jim Eldridge
Illustrations © 2013 David Shephard

The moral right of Jim Eldridge and David Shephard to be
identified as the author and illustrator of this work has been
asserted in accordance with the Copyright, Designs and
Patents Act, 1988

A CIP catalogue record for this book is available
from the British Library upon request

ISBN: 978-1-78112-211-2

Printed in Great Britain by Charlesworth Press

Contents

Chapter 1
Take Cover!

The small hospital block was almost finished. The outer walls had bullet marks on them from attacks by the Taliban, but that hadn't stopped the building work. The British soldiers, engineers and medics in this part of Afghanistan were used to attacks by the Taliban. It was a way of life for them.

Dr Sari Patel was pushing a barrow full of concrete blocks over to the soldiers and local men who were building the walls. She stopped to take a break and watched a few small children laugh and run around among the men. Older children helped their fathers and uncles put the concrete blocks in place.

It was all very different from Sari's work as a doctor back in Birmingham. When she first became a doctor she had never imagined she'd end up pushing blocks around a building site. But this wasn't any old building site. This was a hospital for the people of this small village. It was so important to the village that everyone had come to help build it – soldiers, doctors and local people.

Sari saw Captain Joe MacBride standing looking at the building. He looked deep in thought. Sari walked over to him.

"There's not much more to do now," she said. "Just the roof to go on, and then we can put in the electric cables."

Joe didn't answer. He just stood there with his head to one side, as if he was listening for something.

"What's up?" Sari asked.

"I'm not sure," said Joe. He looked at the rocky desert around them and at the mountains above. Then he looked at the soldiers who were keeping watch behind piles of sandbags. They were a small unit. Joe was the leader, and then there were Sari and two other army medics, four army engineers and six soldiers. Just fourteen of them out here in the desert.

"You think the Taliban are going to attack?" Sari asked.

"I'm thinking it'll be soon," said Joe. "It's been nearly a week since they last attacked. And that was just a small raid."

"I don't understand why they want to stop this hospital being built," Sari said. "It will help the local people."

"But we're building it, and they see us as the enemy," Joe told her.

"This hospital will be for everyone," said Sari. "It doesn't matter if they're on our side or if they're with the Taliban."

Just then there was a whistling sound in the air. At the same time Sari heard a shout from one of the soldiers on guard. "Incoming!" the soldier yelled.

"Take cover!" Joe shouted.

Sari rushed over to the small hospital building. She threw herself in the door just as the blast came from behind her.

Chapter 2
Shot!

The force of the blast pushed Sari forwards and she hit the ground hard. As she struggled to her feet she saw Joe run into the building. He was covered in dust.

"It was an RPG," he told her.

RPG was short for 'Rocket Propelled Grenade'.

The sound of gunshots came from outside. The soldiers were shooting at the Taliban. The Taliban were shooting at the hospital and the small troop of soldiers. Bullets hit the small hospital, but the concrete walls stopped them.

"They're not too close yet," said Joe.

"But they're near enough to hit us with RPGs," Sari said. She looked around. Some of the children had made it into the hospital with their parents. She guessed that others were outside, sheltering behind the building.

Joe headed out with his rifle at the ready. Sari followed him. They made a run for a low wall at the edge of the village. The wall was a mix of sandbags and rocks.

As he ran, Joe used his radio to talk to another solider.

"Call HQ, Giggs," he said. "Tell them we need back-up. We're under attack!"

"Roger, sir!" said Giggs.

Joe and Sari took cover behind the wall and scanned the desert and the mountains with their binoculars. For the moment the Taliban had stopped shooting.

Joe spoke into his radio again.

"Have you seen them?" he asked the guards.

"There's a small group about 1km to the south, Captain," one of the soldiers replied. "Behind those rocks near that line of trees."

Even as he spoke, there was a small blast, and smoke came up from behind the rocks near the line of trees. Then there was the same whistling sound as another RPG headed towards them.

Sari and Joe ducked down behind the wall, and the soldiers ducked behind their sandbags.

WHOOMPPFFFF!

This time the RPG smashed into the top of the front wall of the hospital, where it tore off part of the top layer of blocks. Screams came from inside the building and children and parents rushed out from their hiding places. Some ran to join Joe and Sari and the soldiers behind the wall. Others ran for the village.

A burst of gunshots came from the Taliban fighters hidden behind the rocks. The British soldiers shot back straight away. Their bullets tore into the trees and sent chips of rock flying in the air.

There was a howl of pain from the village that made Sari look round. A man and a woman were sitting by two small crumpled shapes on the ground. The woman was crying and howling.

"Cover me!" Sari yelled.

Sari waved to another medic called Adam, and the two of them ran over to the family. They stayed low as they ran. Behind them, Joe and the soldiers fired a steady stream of shots at the rocks where the Taliban were hidden.

At last, Sari and Adam got to the family. A boy of about 10 was on the ground, crying. Blood was soaking through his trousers. Sari tore open the cloth. There was a large wound in his leg, just above his knee. Blood was pumping out of it.

"Take care of him!" Sari said to Adam. "I'll help the little girl!"

Adam tore a strip of cloth from the boy's trousers and tied it tightly around his leg, just above the wound. Straight away the blood began to stop pumping.

"I'll take him inside," said Adam.

"My medical bag's in our truck," Sari told him.

Adam nodded. He picked up the boy and began to run to the village. He stayed low as he ran, like before, in case any more bullets came flying in. But the soldiers were doing a good job of holding the Taliban back.

Sari looked at the little girl. She was about five years old. She lay face down on the ground and she wasn't moving. There was blood on the back of her dress. Sari felt for the pulse in her neck. It was weak, but it was there.

Sari tore open the back of the girl's dress where it was stained with blood. There was a wound in her back, just below her heart. Sari put her hand round and felt the front of the girl's chest. No blood. No wound. That meant the bullet was still inside the girl.

'This is a problem,' Sari thought. 'If the bullet's stuck near the girl's heart and I move her, the bullet could move too. It could kill her. On the other hand, if we leave her here, she'll die anyway.'

'I must operate,' Sari thought. 'I've got to get that bullet out.'

Chapter 3
Under Fire

Sari looked up at the girl's mother and father. Both looked terrified.

Sari had learned to speak Pushtu before she came to Afghanistan. "I'm going to carry your daughter into the village," she told the girl's parents. "I need a room with a table, and hot water. Lots of it."

The girl's father nodded and ran towards the village. Sari picked up the girl and followed him. The girl's tiny body was so light. The girl's mother ran along behind.

....

Over behind the low wall of sandbags and rocks, Captain Joe MacBride fired another round towards the rocks where the Taliban fighters were hiding. Since that second RPG had hit the hospital building, they had been very quiet.

"Any sign of them?" he called into his radio.

"No, sir," came the reply.

'I reckon they're on the move,' Joe thought. 'They're creeping along the gully behind those rocks. They'll launch another attack from a different spot.'

Just as he thought it, there was a shout from one of the soldiers.

"RPG, Captain! From the south east!"

Then there was the whistle of the RPG coming through the air. This one slammed into the ground just in front of the wall. When it blew up, sand and rocks flew into the air and rained down on the soldiers.

'That was close,' Joe thought. 'Too close!'

"They've moved, sir!" another soldier shouted. "That RPG came from the south east, behind that patch of rocks."

Then they heard a burst of gunfire, and a shower of bullets sailed over their heads and smashed into the concrete walls of the hospital building.

"They've split into two groups!" Joe yelled. "Those shots came from the south west! Open fire in both directions!"

The soldiers opened fire as he told them. Joe saw a Taliban fighter stand up behind the rocks and aim his gun at them.

Bang!

Joe fired. His shot sent the Taliban fighter tumbling out of sight.

"Any word back yet from HQ, Giggs?" Joe asked.

"A chopper's on its way, sir!" Giggs told him. "They reckon they'll be here in 20 minutes!"

'20 minutes,' thought Joe. With Sari and Adam gone to help the wounded kids, there were just ten of them left to defend the village. He wondered how many Taliban fighters were out there. From the number of shots he guessed there were at least 15 of them in each group. 30 in total. Maybe more.

It was going to be a long 20 minutes.

Chapter 4
Must Operate!

Sari spread a blanket on the table and laid the tiny girl down on her front. They were inside one of the small mud houses near the hospital. The girl's parents were there, and so were a number of other people who had come into the house to help or just to watch. Gunfire roared outside.

Adam came in with Sari's medical bag.

"The little boy's OK," he said. "I stitched up his wound and put on a bandage. I've given him painkillers." He looked at the still body of the small girl. "How is she?" he asked.

"The bullet's still inside her," Sari said. "I need to find it and take it out. The trouble is, I don't know how near her heart it is. Or it could be in her lung. It would be hard to operate in a proper hospital. Doing it here, in a house with no electricity, and no proper kit ... It's so dangerous. But I don't think we have a choice."

Adam looked at the tiny girl.

"Will I give her a shot to keep her knocked out?" he asked.

"Yes," said Sari. "We can't risk her waking up while I'm opening her up. We need to keep her still."

A man with a big grey beard stepped forward and said something in Pushtu. Sari nodded and answered him.

"What was that about?" Adam asked.

"He's a local healer," Sari said. "He says he's got some herbs that will keep the wound clean and help her get better."

"But we've got proper drugs," Adam said.

"It's best if we work together," Sari told him. "These people know this girl and her family. They know what's best for her."

Then Sari turned and spoke to the girl's parents and the rest of the people in their own language.

"What were you saying?" Adam asked as he filled a needle, ready to inject the girl.

"I told them we're going to open her up and take the bullet out, if we can," Sari said. "You should learn Pushtu," she added.

"Yes, I should," Adam agreed. "I think we're going to be here for a long time."

Adam pressed the point of the needle into the girl's arm and injected the drug into her.

Sari tied a mask over her nose and mouth so she wouldn't breathe germs into the wound. Adam did the same.

The villagers stood around the table and shone torches at the body of the girl so that the doctors could see what they were doing.

Sari and Adam washed their hands in hot water. Then Sari picked up a scalpel from her medical kit. She held it just over the bullet

wound and got ready to make her first cut. But just then, there was a blast outside that shook the whole house. An RPG had blown up just outside the house. People fell to the floor. Bits of dried clay fell off the walls onto the floor. Dust choked them all.

Some of the people in the room rushed out to find shelter in places further away from the battle. The girl's parents and the man with the grey beard stayed, their eyes on the still body of the little girl.

"Are you still OK to do this?" Adam asked.

Sari nodded. "Let's just hope the next one doesn't come in here."

Chapter 5
The Bullet

Outside by the wall, Joe looked over to where the RPG had landed. He swore. It had blown up right by the house where Sari was operating on the little qirl.

"We need to put the guy firing those RPGs out of action," Joe said to the other soldiers.

"Zubu and Redding, use the mortar. Everyone else, cover them!"

The soldiers opened fire right away. Their bullets smashed into the rocks behind which the Taliban fighters were hiding.

Zubu and Redding ran to the mortar. It had already been set up in case of attack. Zubu and Redding loaded a small bomb into the barrel and took aim at the rocks where the Taliban were firing the RPGs. Then they fired.

The small bomb from the mortar sailed into the air and blew up just in front of the rocks. Joe was watching through his binoculars.

"Send the next one three metres further," he ordered.

The soldiers fired the mortar again. This time the small bomb landed exactly where Joe wanted it. There was a blast and smoke and flames flew up from behind the rocks.

"Good one!" called Joe.

The trouble was, they didn't know if they'd scored a hit on the launcher the Taliban were using to launch the RPGs. They might have moved it somewhere else, just before the bomb landed.

. . . .

34

Inside the house, Sari cut into the wound on the girl's back and peeled back the skin and flesh. The villagers held the torches up high so Sari could see what she was doing.

Adam kept an eye on the girl's pulse and her breathing.

All the time they were aware of the shots and the blasts going on outside, and the building shaking.

Sari called one of the village men over and told him to point his torch into the open wound. She peered in.

Yes, there it was – the bullet.

It had hit one of the little girl's ribs and gone upwards. It was very, very near her heart.

Now the big problem was the girl's blood. It was seeping up through the wound and filling the small but deep hole in the girl's body, hiding the bullet.

"Adam, I need help here," said Sari. "We need to get the blood out of the wound so I can see the bullet."

"There's no power," Adam said. "I don't know how to do it without electricity."

"Think of something!" Sari snapped. "I know – there's a little water pump in the truck that works with a battery. That should suck the blood out."

Adam rushed out to the truck. As he opened the door of the hut, a Taliban bullet almost hit him. It smashed into the door an inch from his head.

"Help!" Adam yelled into his radio. "I need cover!"

Straight away the soldiers opened fire. Their bullets were like a shield over Adam, keeping the Taliban back so they couldn't fire on him.

38

Adam ran to the truck and climbed in the back. He found the pump and a piece of clear plastic tube and jumped back down again. As he ran back to the house a stray bullet smacked into the wall just over his head.

"Got it!" he said.

Adam and Sari connected the clear plastic pipe to the pump, and put the other end into the open wound. Blood began to be sucked up into the clear plastic tube.

"Good," said Sari. She picked up a pair of long tweezers. "Right, I'm going in."

But just as she said the words, there was a blast from above their heads, and the roof fell in.

Chapter 6
Direct Hit

"Zubu! Redding! Come on!" Joe smashed his fist into his leg.

"We're on it, sir!" Zubu yelled back. The next second he and Redding fired another bomb from the mortar. This one came down right on the place the RPG had been launched from.

There were screams and shouts from behind the rocks as the mortar bomb blew up.

"Sari, what's happening?" Joe yelled into his headset.

He turned and looked at the house where Sari had been operating on the little girl. Flames blazed from the roof and smoke poured out the doors and windows. The Taliban rocket had made a direct hit on the house.

"Sari!" Joe called again.

There was a splutter through his headset, and then Sari's voice struggled to say the words: "We're OK."

Joe was shocked. How could they be okay?
The house had taken a direct hit.

"Hold the line!" Joe yelled to his men. Then
he ran towards the house, keeping as low as he
could. Behind him the soldiers fired rapidly to
cover him as he ran.

In a few seconds he had reached the house.
Thick smoke was still pouring out the door and
windows. There was no way that there could be
anyone alive in there.

Joe pulled his scarf over his mouth and
nose, and ran inside.

A little light came in from the hole in the roof. The floor was covered in beams and clay. There was no sign of Sari, or the girl, or Adam, or the family, or even the table. Any furniture there was in the room was smashed or burning.

Then, through the smoke, Joe saw another open door leading out to the back of the house. He ran across and out the door. An amazing sight met his eyes.

Sari and Adam were bending over the girl, who lay still on a blanket on the table. Broken wood and clay from the roof lay all around her. Sari and Adam were filthy with dust and smoke, and there were bits of dried mud and wood in their hair and on their clothes.

The family stood round, shining torches on the little girl on the table, even though it was daylight.

Adam had a pump that seemed to be sucking blood from a wound in the little girl's back.

Sari was pressing carefully in the open wound with something that looked like tweezers. She pulled the tweezers out, and Joe saw that there was a metal object trapped in the blades. Sari dropped the metal object on the table. Then she saw him.

"Joe!" she called. "Get my medical case from the house. We didn't have time to bring it."

Joe ran back inside the house. Because of the hole in the roof, most of the smoke had cleared away. Joe saw Sari's medical case on the floor. He grabbed it and ran back outside.

"Adam, cut some bandage!" Sari ordered.

While Adam cut the bandage, Sari set to work sewing up the flesh on the inside of the wound. As she sewed, she told the villagers to go and get her some hot water.

"What do you want me to do to help?" asked Joe.

"You can stop the Taliban shooting us while I sew her up," said Sari.

Joe grinned. "Leave it to me."

Chapter 7
Rescue

Joe ran back to the low wall where his soldiers were keeping up a steady stream of fire at the Taliban. Zubu and Redding were using the mortar to fire mortar bombs at the Taliban lines.

"Sir, we're running low on ammo!" shouted the soldier nearest to Joe.

"How much have we got?" Joe asked.

"At this rate, enough for about four minutes."

Joe swore. Where was that helicopter they'd been promised?

And just then he heard them coming. He turned and saw them – two helicopter gunships, coming down lower.

'Let's hope they don't start firing too soon,' he thought. 'If they see Sari and Adam and the villagers at the back of the house, they might think they're Taliban attackers. Sari and Adam

are both covered in dirt, and there's nothing to show they're medics.'

"Giggs!" he called to the radio operator. "Patch me in to the choppers!"

"Doing it now, sir!" called back Giggs.

Then Joe heard the helicopter pilot's voice though his headset.

"Delta Victor 2 to ground position, do you read? Over."

"I read you!" Joe answered. "Taliban south of our position, on mountain. Do not attack people near houses. Repeat, do not attack people near houses."

"Got you!" came the pilot's voice.

By now, both helicopters were right above the village, flying low. They flew over Joe and the soldiers, so low that their rotors made a sandstorm. And then Joe heard the sound of rapid shots as the helicopters opened up with their guns on the Taliban. Their bullets poured down like deadly rain.

....

Sari put the final stitches to the wound she'd sewn up on the little girl's back. Adam checked her pulse and breathing. All of a sudden, Joe appeared by the table. In the sky, the gunfire from the helicopters carried on.

"How is she?" Joe asked.

"She's weak, but she'll live," said Sari. "Now the choppers are here, they should be able to take me to a hospital where I can make sure she's OK."

Joe looked back at what was left of the house.

"How did you get out of there?" he asked.

"We grabbed the table and lifted it out," Sari said. "Adam and I never stopped looking after the girl. And outside, there was no roof to fall on us." She cocked her head and listened. The gunfire had stopped.

"Sounds like the battle's over," she said.

Joe nodded. "For the moment," he said. "Until the Taliban come back and try and hit us again."

Through his headset, he heard one of the pilots speak. "Bandits eliminated," the pilot said. "We're finished here. Are there any wounded we need to get out?"

"A little girl and a little boy," said Joe. "They need to get to a hospital – fast."

"We haven't got a doctor on board," the pilot said.

"No need," said Joe. "We've got one here. She'll go with you."

"Roger that," said the pilot. "Bring them along."

They looked up and saw the two helicopters land on the flat plain.

"Will you be OK, doctor?" Joe asked.

Sari nodded.

"I'll get the two kids settled, then come back." She looked at the shattered buildings around them. She nodded towards the scarred and battled hospital building and smiled.

"We've got a hospital to build."

Our books are tested
for children and young people by
children and young people.

Thanks to everyone who consulted on
a manuscript for their time and effort in
helping us to make our books better
for our readers.